W9-CMF-670

2015

The Three Little Pigs

CARAMEL TREE

The Three Brothers Leave Home

There were three little pigs named Alex, John, and Newton. They left their mother's home. Each pig had a little money.

Alex was a lazy pig. He saw a donkey selling straw.

"This is perfect!" he said. "Straw is cheap. It is also easy to build a house."

Alex finished building his house in three hours. Then he lay down to rest.

John ran to the market and bought an axe.
Then he went to the forest. He chopped down
six trees.

John built his house in three days.
He worked hard. But he was not smart.
John sat in his shoddy home.

The Big Bad Wolf

Newton saw his brothers' houses. The straw house was weak. The wooden house was shoddy.

Newton made a plan to build his house better and stronger.

Newton saw a shop selling bricks.
He bought two hundred bricks.
    After three weeks, Newton had built
a beautiful brick house.

One morning, the Big Bad Wolf saw Alex's house. *'I will blow down that straw house and eat the little pig,'* thought the Wolf.

"Little pig, little pig, let me in," shouted the Wolf. Alex was scared.

"Are you crazy?" yelled Alex. "You will eat me if I let you in!"

The Wolf huffed and puffed and
blew the house down.
　　Alex ran to John's house.
　　'Oh good,' thought the Wolf, *'now
I can eat two little pigs.'*

Huff and Puff,
Huff and Puff

"Little pigs, little pigs, let me in!" he shouted.
"No way!" cried the brothers.
The Wolf huffed and puffed. The house shook.

Alex and John were scared.
The Wolf huffed and puffed again.
The shoddy wooden house blew away.

The two little pigs ran for Newton's house. Alex was fat and ran slowly. The Wolf caught Alex and tied him up. But he wanted to eat all three pigs.

Newton was not scared. He knew his house was strong. Every day he worked hard carrying bricks. Now he was very big and strong, too.

The Wolf huffed and puffed.
He huffed and puffed.
And he huffed and puffed again.
But the brick house did not blow down.

4 POW!

The Wolf was tired. Suddenly, out came Newton. The Wolf was surprised to see a big strong pig.

POW!

Newton punched the Wolf. The Wolf went flying over the hills. He never came back.

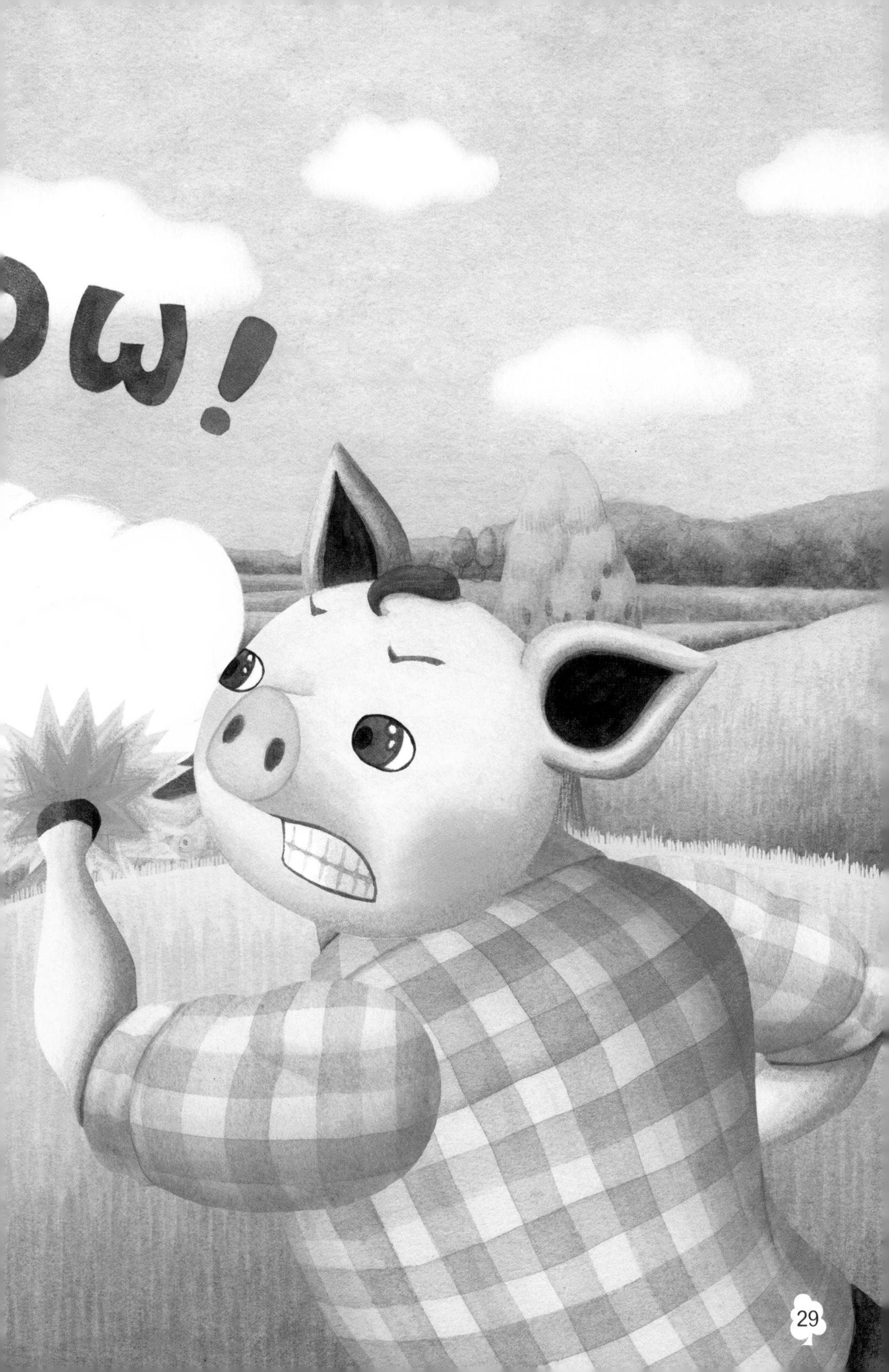
ow!

"My brothers," said Newton. "You were almost eaten today. Alex, you were lazy. John, you were not smart. You two will build your own brick houses."

Newton sat inside his warm home. Every day he watched his brothers carry bricks. He was very happy.